This edition published by Parragon Books Ltd in 2016
and distributed by

Parragon Inc.
440 Park Avenue South, 13th Floor
New York, NY 10016
www.parragon.com

Copyright © Parragon Books Ltd 2016

ISBN 978-1-4748-3300-4
Printed in China

Sweet Dream
Bedtime Stories

PaRragon

Bath · New York · Cologne · Melbourne · Delhi
Hong Kong · Shenzhen · Singapore

Contents

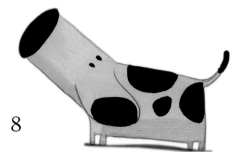

For Daniel and the ba, from your Granja

Written by Malachy Doyle   Illustrated by Barroux

Milo loves his owner.

She's a girl called Molly Brown.

But Milo's nose loves food the most ...

It leads him all round town.

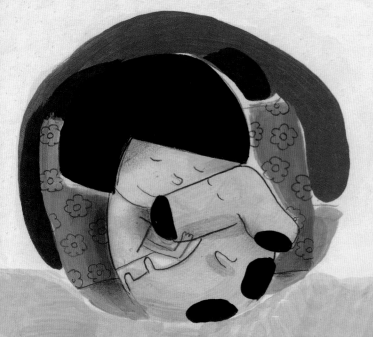

10

For Milo's nose is a nose
that knows—it knows
when food is near.
When it smells a smell,
the nose soon shows
poor Milo where to steer!

Molly's heading out with Mom.

Milo runs.

BARK! BARK!

But the nose has sniffed a **SANDWICH** moving quickly through the park!

Where that nose goes, Milo goes ...

SPLASH! So now he's paddling through a pond!

Then his nose smells a smell of which he's really rather fond!

13

It's coming from that office block.

Oh my—it does smell fine!

The nose has caught a sniff of cheese and pies and fries—WHERE'S MINE?

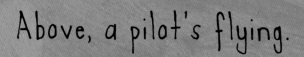

Above, a pilot's flying.

Is that **PIZZA** on a plate?

The nose that knows
drags Milo, but—
OH NO!—
he's just too late!

He clings on to the 'copter
as it flies off through the air ...

19

But then his nose smells ...

20

... crunchy, munchy **APPLES** over there!

21

They're in that massive rocket—he'll just grab one, then he'll go.

He sneaks in, but the doors close ...

SIX

FIVE

FOUR

THREE TWO ONE

WHOA!

23

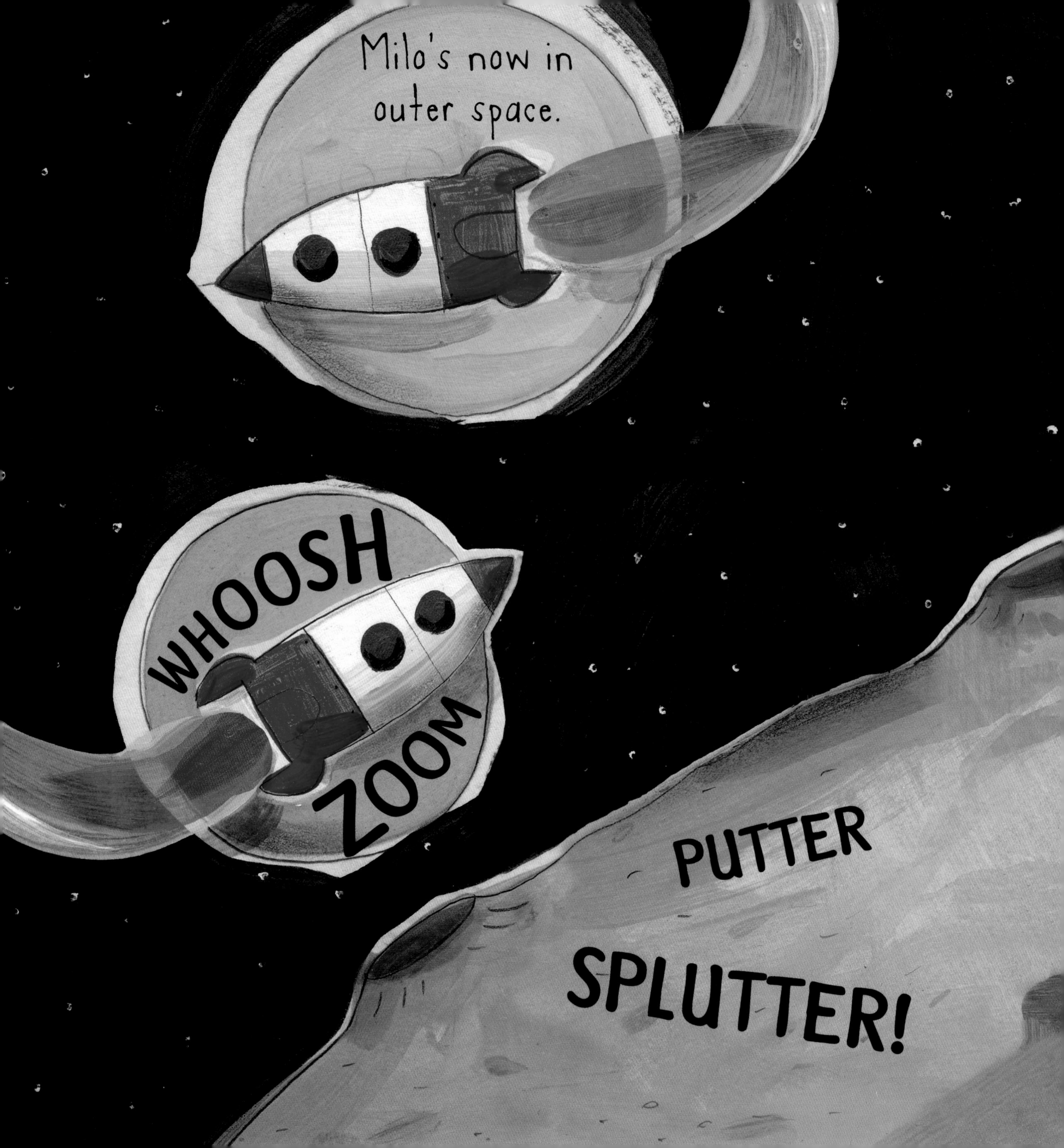
Milo's now in outer space.
WHOOSH
ZOOM
PUTTER
SPLUTTER!

Out he climbs, and finds the moon is made of **PEANUT BUTTER!**

He tries to lick, but then his nose smells something oh so nice!

It's miles and miles away, but it smells just like paradise!

His nose, it knows what's cooking—
it's his favorite thing to eat ...
Cooking on a barbecue, it's yummy, sizzling **MEAT!**

"Hey! You're back!" cries Molly.
"Wherever did you go?"
Milo wags his tail, but
she will never ever know!

27

Molly is just glad he's home and gives him

ONE HUGE TREAT!

Milo's glad to be back, too,
and glad—at last—to eat.

So Milo, he might wander.
Yes Milo, he might roam.
But Milo's nose is a nose that knows
and will always lead him to ...

MOLLY, FOOD, and **HOME!**

Written and illustrated by
Beverley Gooding

This book is dedicated
to Mr David Rae

Max
and
Tallulah

a little love story

Max loved Tallulah

with all his heart.

But he was too shy to tell her.

38

Max needed a way to make Tallulah notice him. So he decided to give her a present. He picked her favorite fruit, balanced it on a lily leaf, and pushed it carefully along the river.

But just before Max reached Tallulah, the leaf started to sink! All of the fruit fell into the water and floated away.

Max needed another plan.

That night, by the light
of the Moon, Max practiced a
daring dance!

When the Sun began
to rise, he went to
find Tallulah.

Tallulah was in the forest
looking for juicy leaves.

Max was certain that his daring
dance would get her attention.

He stepped forward ...

He tapped his hoof ...

He leaped into the sky ...

And he twirled,
faster and faster!

46

Surely Tallulah would notice him now?

But Tallulah was so busy eating
that she didn't see Max or any
of his daring dance.

Max needed a new idea.

He gathered leaves and flowers and insects of every size and color.

Max was going to make the most magnificent hat Tallulah had ever seen!

Surely that would impress her?

But when Max appeared in his magnificent hat ...

... Tallulah was so startled that she ran away!

Max had not meant to frighten Tallulah.
What could he do now?

Suddenly, Max saw his reflection
in the water, and he had the

greatest idea of all!

He was going to be ...

JUST MAX!

Max smiled at Tallulah ...

... and Tallulah smiled back!

Written by Beth Shoshan

Illustrated by Petra Brown

Where you go...
I go.

The Sun comes up and smiles on us
And starts to warm the early day.

My sleepy eyes can see you move.

Where you go ... I go.

Then out we dash, to leap and play
And scramble in the morning Sun.

You push some leaves
aside for me ...

(Hey Mom! Hey, look!
Guess who's a tree?!)

Let's go have fun, and mess about.

When you play ...
I play.

(Oh no!)
The skies turn gray,
It starts to rain,
And you just want to
keep me dry ...
(Thanks Mom!)

I run and shelter under you.

Where you are ... I am.

And as we walk on, trunk in trunk,
And talk about the things I'll do ...

(You'll teach me, Mom ...
you always do.)

You tell me just
how much you care,

('I love you Mom,' I sing to you!)

What you love ... I love.

Then when it's time to scrub me clean,
We'll splish and splosh and splash about.

You wash away my bathtime fears,

(Just don't forget behind my ears!)

When you smile ... I smile.

And when the day has reached its end
And both of us are getting tired,

I'll snuggle up and feel your warmth.
When you sleep ... I sleep.

Written by Peter Bently

Illustrated by Rob McPhillips

"Say Please,
Little Bear"

Daddy Bear and Little Bear were on the way to Kindergarten.
But Little Bear kept wandering off.

"Keep hold of my
hand, Little Bear!"
said Daddy Bear.

"Go gently,
Little Bear!"
said Daddy Bear.

But Little Bear didn't listen.

"Little Bear, it isn't nice to snatch!"

"It's better when
we share, Little Bear,"
said Daddy Bear.

Later, Daddy Bear took Little Bear to
Little Bunny's birthday party.
They went shopping on the way.
"Please hold my hand, Little Bear!"
said Daddy wearily.

Then something in the shop window
gave Daddy Bear an idea.
"Look, Little Bear," he said.
"That mouse wants
to speak to us!"

"Mouse wants to come to the party too, Little Bear," said Daddy Bear. "But he hates to be late!"

They reached Little Bunny's party on time.
Mouse whispered in Daddy Bear's ear.

"Mouse says, excuse me, please."

Little Bear ran to play on the train.
Mouse whispered in Daddy Bear's ear.
"Mouse says,
can she have
a ride on the
train, please?"

Little Bear snatched the popcorn from his friends.
Mouse whispered in Daddy Bear's ear.
"Mouse says, would *you* like some popcorn, Bunny and Mole?"

When it was time to go,
Little Bear stood silently
on the doorstep.
"Mouse says, thank you
for having me,"
said Daddy.

Little Bear looked at Mouse. Then he looked at Daddy Bear. Then he looked at Little Bunny's mom, and said, "And thank you for having me."

"Oh, thank you for coming,
Little Bear,"
smiled Little Bunny's mom.

"You and Mouse can come
and play anytime."

"Mouse likes the way
you said thank you,"
said Daddy Bear.

"And so do I."

The story ends.

The sharing begins.

Written by Jillian Harker
Illustrated by Gill McLean

I Wish ...

Benji sat on the bed, feeling a little bit lonely. He was new here, and he hadn't seen anyone else in the bedroom.

He watched a moonbeam slip through a gap in the curtains and slide across the bed.

"I wish I had someone to play with," he whispered.

"Did I hear someone say they wanted to play?" asked a voice. The lid of the toy box flew open, and out climbed a dangly-legged, spotted horse.
"Hi, I'm Dottie … and I love to play!"

Dottie jumped onto the bed and began to bounce up and down.

"Where did you come from?" she asked.

"From the birthday party," replied Benji. "I was a present."

"Did someone mention a party?" A friendly-looking monkey poked his head around the curtain. "Why weren't Rosie and I invited?"

A floppy-eared rabbit appeared beside him.

"Max and I love parties!" Rosie the rabbit told Benji. "And so does Humph."

She stared at the toy box. A loud yawn came from inside. Then a bright blue hippo slowly lifted his head.

Party!

"A party!" said Humph. "That means food. And I'm hungry! Is there anything left to eat?"

"I think there are some cupcakes in the kitchen," replied Benji. "But do you think we should … ?"

But Humph was already
out the door!

"Oh!" said Benji, looking at the
other toys. "Should we go after him?"

Benji was bumping down the stairs after Humph when Dottie zoomed past.

"This is fun!" she neighed.

"Wait for me!" called Benji.

WHEEEE!

In the kitchen, Humph was about to take a bite out of a leftover cupcake. The candle was already halfway into his mouth.

Benji grabbed it just in time.

'Excuse me,' he explained, 'but you aren't meant to eat that bit.'

'Thanks, Benji. You're smart. I wish I knew things like that,' grumbled Humph.

Before Benji could explain about the candle, he heard Dottie and Rosie yell loudly. They were staring at a large black shape outside the kitchen window.

They grabbed Benji and held on tight.

"It's just a cat," Benji said. "No need to worry."

"Phew," sighed Rosie with relief.

"I wish I could be as brave as you, Benji," laughed Dottie.

"That cat will stay outside, won't it?" whispered
Max. They all looked to Benji for reassurance. Max
had crept across the room and hidden under the table.
Humph's knees were shaking.

There was a squeaking noise and then a loud **clatter!**

"Don't worry, that's just the cat coming into the kitchen," explained Benji. But Humph and Dottie, Max and Rosie had all raced out through the kitchen door and disappeared up the stairs as fast as their legs could carry them!

Benji found them all back in the bedroom.
It took some time to persuade them to come out.

"Benji, will you always be here
to look after us?" Dottie asked him.

Benji gave a tiny little smile. It was nice to
feel wanted.

"Of course," he replied.

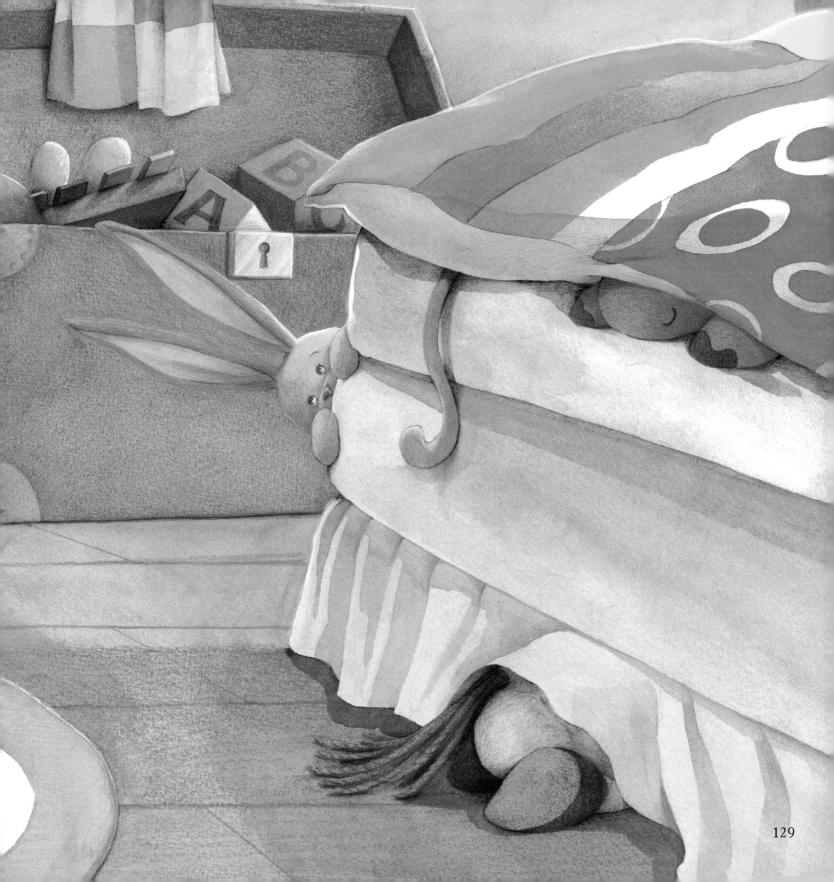

Humph was tired from their adventure. "How am I going to sleep when I'm so hungry?" he sniffed, settling back down on the bed.

Dottie and Rosie giggled. They danced around on the bed. Max joined in.

"Why don't we all play in the yard tomorrow?"
Rosie suggested.
"What's your yard like?" asked Benji.
"I'll show you," said Dottie, and she helped Benji
up so he could look out the window.

"Wow!" he said. "It looks really exciting.
Are you going to play in the yard, Humph?"

"Humph!" said Humph sleepily. "It's such a long
way to the yard. I might just take a little nap instead."

Benji smiled at his new sleepy friend.

Dottie jumped back onto the bed and started to bounce. Benji looked up at the Moon. He had a feeling that he wouldn't be lonely any more.

"I wish that tomorrow will be as much fun as today," he whispered.

Then Benji turned to
his new friends and took
a huge leap, and began
to bounce on the bed.
"Here's to friends!"
he laughed.

Written by Annie Baker

Illustrated by Barroux

I LOVE YOU WHEN ...

I love you when it's warm and sunny.

I love you when you're being funny.

I love you when it's wet outside.

I love you when you want to hide.

145

146

I even love you when you're sneezy.

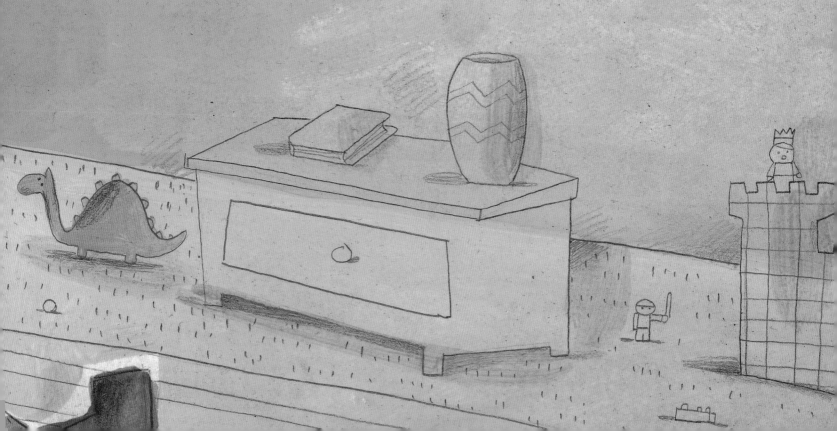

I love you when we rush to and fro,

and I love you when there's nowhere to go.

I love you when you're feeling sleepy.

I love you when you're sad and weepy.

I love you when you giggle ...

when you wiggle ...

when you wriggle ...

155

I love you when you're snuggly.

I love you when you're huggly.

I love you when you say, "I love you too."

But mostly I love you **whenever**
I'm with you.